The Voice

The Voice

MISS CHEYENNE MITCHELL

LitPrime Solutions
485c US Highway 1 South
Suite 100
Iselin, NJ 08830
www.litprime.com
Phone: 1-800-981-9893

Published by LitPrime Solutions: 09/13/2024

ISBN: 979-8-88703-398-3(sc)
ISBN: 979-8-88703-399-0(e)

Library of Congress Control Number: 2024916428

It was an unusually warm, beautiful evening in Laycock, the town where I'd lived all of my life. Christmas was coming soon. A little snow was still covering the houses as well as the ground. It was much too beautiful for the occasion at hand. My house had been cleaned from top to bottom for the event to come that night. I was never good at housekeeping. The furniture was sparkling and the hardwood floors were gleaming. My house was filled to capacity with people that I knew and loved.

I watched as various members of my family chatted with my neighbors and friends. They were all going to a funeral. The children seemed to be oblivious to the sadness and sorrow around them. However, my daughter, Tanda, was nowhere to be seen.

She had just turned seven years old, and it was strange that she wasn't playing with the other children. They were enjoying themselves playing a game of hide and seek. I couldn't help but smile.

"Come on, Traya!" Suddenly I heard a familiar voice speaking to me again. One I had heard once before tonight. "It's time for us to leave." "Just a little while longer," I replied. I never did turn around so I didn't know who was talking to me. When I did no one was there.

All I could think about was finding my little girl. It wasn't like her not to be with the other children. She was very outgoing, and friendly. I realized that something must be wrong.

I made my way upstairs past the guests to see if she was in her bedroom. When I opened her bedroom door there she was lying across her bed sobbing softly. "Tanda, honey," I said, "it's Mommy." I had no idea why she was so dispirited.

"It's going to be alright, honey," I told her softly, "you'll see." She dried her eyes with the back of her hand. With a couple of left over sniffles she got off of the bed, and smoothed out the dress that she was wearing.

I walked over to her and put my arm around her shoulders. Then I kissed her gently on her forehead. "I'll be okay, Mommy," she said barely above a whisper, looking toward the bedroom ceiling.

I tried not to worry about it, but she didn't seem to be comforted by me. "She's upset about something," I thought. I watched her as she went downstairs to join the others.

"We must go now, Traya." I heard the voice again. "We've been here

too long as it is. Please, let's just leave." "Just a bit longer," I
said to the unknown person. "What's the hurry?" I headed back
downstairs because I wanted to make sure that Tanda was alright.

Jason Whims, a somber, little man who was the Undertaker in our
town, had just arrived. He began to organize family members, and
friends for the ride to the church. I watched as they lined up when
he called out the names for the designated cars from the list of
names that my mother had given to him. I knew the routine well. It
was the way that our family always did things when a family member
passed away.

The way that they did things for funerals in my mother's time. The
service was held at night, and the burial would be held on the
following morning. They lined up according to the closest members of
the deceased. Then my mother started to sob softly. "Oh, Mom," I said
soothingly, "please don't cry. You have to be strong."

My mother's name was, Diana, and she was a widow. My father died of
Pneumonia two years ago. I was one of four siblings and the only
girl. Therefore, my mother and I were close. We both had the same
thick, dark brown hair, brown complexion, and big, dark brown eyes.
My brothers resembled my mother, too. My family was so proud of me
when I graduated from college, being the first one. I found a job
right away. It was as an Assistant Television Programmer with one of
the local T.V. stations.

My mother was even more proud of me when I decided to have a child
without the benefit of marriage. I was kind of surprised by that.
She came from an era when things like that were not done. An era that
believed in marriage *before* having children.

I didn't want to marry, Ashly, Tanda's father, for reasons that my
family was well aware of. Ashly had a problem controlling his anger,
and would beat on me. I lost count of how many times I was
hospitalized when we were a couple.

When Tanda was five years old I decided to end the relationship
once and for all. I didn't hear from Ashly for nearly a year after
that. He never bothered to pay child support. I had to haul him into
court. In fact he never cared about what was best or good for Tanda
or for me. He was all for himself. A very selfish man.

Suddenly out of nowhere he wanted to be part of Tanda's life. At
first I had mixed feelings about it, but in the end I relented. I
felt that it wasn't fair to Tanda not to allow her father, as sorry
as he was, to be in her life.

They developed a good relationship with each other. Therefore, over
time he and I decided to give our own relationship another try. My
mother warned me that it was a terrible mistake, but I wouldn't
listen to her. I felt that I had to give Ashly a chance. Many times
I wished that I had listened to my mother. I didn't realize that she
could see farther down the road than I could.

When we got to the church it was very crowded. Every pew was full.
I think everybody in Laycock came out for the funeral. There were
people standing in front of the church talking. So I decided to stay
outside for a while, too.

"I don't understand how something like this could've happened,"
sobbed Myrna sadly. She was another Assistant Programmer at the
station where I worked. "She didn't deserve this shit! I hope they
catch that dirty, rotten bastard and give him the death sentence for
what he did to her." I had no idea who she was talking about.

 "I know what you mean," replied Eddie who was our Mail Carrier. "She
was a damn nice lady. How could something like this happen?" He
shook his head sorrowfully. As if he couldn't believe the terrible,
and tragic thing that had happened to the woman whose funeral we were
attending.

I went back inside the church when they did. There were so many
people crying. I never did go to the front of the church where the
body laid in its' casket. There were so many beautiful flowers. I was
hoping someone would notice the nice dress that I had on. It was
light blue, my favorite color.

The scars on my body from the last beating I had taken from Ashly
couldn't be seen. They were covered very well with makeup. I was so
glad. It would have been very embarrassing to my family and I for
people to see the terrible scars that I had. I don't think anyone
even noticed how nicely my hair was done. It was beautifully done by
Minerva Westin, our neighborhood Beautician. She had been mine and
my mother's Hairdresser for many years. I was a little disappointed.
But I knew that everyone was trying to deal with their grief. They
could've cared less what I looked like.

"Traya, please." It was the voice again. "We've got to leave here.
We can't stay. It's time for us to go." "Please," I begged, "just a
little longer." I still didn't know who was talking to me, but it was
a female voice, and a voice that I was familiar with. Mysteriously,
for some reason I couldn't recognize whose voice it was.

Miss Ally Bascome was singing the song Ave. Maria. It was my
favorite hymn, and I wasn't even Catholic. It was beautiful and she

had a wonderful voice. When she was finished singing they covered
the face of the body with a handkerchief. That was also the custom at
our family funerals. Reverend Marsh began to give the Eulogy.

He was a wonderful man, and my family and I knew him for many
years. The Reverend came to my mother's house for dinner on many
occasions even before my father died. My mind began to wander while
he was talking. I started thinking about my life and particularly
about my past.

"I can't understand why you would want to be bothered with a man
like that, Tray," my mother told me one day when Tanda and I were
visiting her. Of course she was referring to Ashly. And the fact that
I decided to try to make another go of our volatile relationship.

"I think he's changed, Mom," I told her confidently. "I really do."
"A man like that never changes, Traya," she said inimically. "Never!
I think you're making a terrible mistake and you will regret it."
"Oh, Mom," I assured her, "everything is going to be okay, you'll
see." She never once believed that and I didn't know how right she
was. My mother was wise and experienced. She knew things that I had
yet to learn.

My older brothers, Connell, and Mark were there at the time.
"Well," Connell told me with umbrage, "if it's not okay let me know.
Please." My brothers were always waiting for any excuse to beat the
hell out of Ashly. They couldn't stand him. I had to hold them back
from hurting Ashly quite a few times. Mark had a smirk on his face
that let me know he agreed with Connell without saying a word.

Ashly Waring, my daughter's father, moved in with Tanda and I a
year ago. Things were nice between us for a long time. We got along
great. He treated Tanda and I very good. I should have known that it
was just a matter of time. As my mother portended to me, one night
the inevitable happened.

Ashly promised that he would never touch another drop of whiskey.
He was mean, pugnacious, and cruel when he was drinking. He wouldn't
stop until he was drunk, and out of control. One night he came home
as drunk as he could be.

I had been waiting dinner for him that night for over three hours.
When he didn't come right home from work I began to get a familiar
daunting feeling in my gut that hadn't been there for a long time.
Something in the back of my mind told me to take Tanda and leave. But
I didn't do it.

I put everything away, put Tanda to bed, and went to bed myself.

Ashly came home and wanted to play with Tanda. Who by that time was
sound asleep in her bed. I had been too fearful to go to sleep.

     I wouldn't allow him to awaken Tanda. It was after midnight. It was
all the excuse that he needed to fly into a rage and beat me up.
After that I was on my way to the hospital. I had three, cracked
ribs, two, black eyes, and another severe concussion.

     All three of my brothers came over to my house, and threw Ashly out
on his head. But not before they beat him to a bloody pulp. He ended
up in the same hospital right along with me. And he was in there for
two weeks. My brothers warned him never to come near me or Tanda
again. I guess out of fear of my brothers Ashly stayed away. But he
started stalking me.

     He followed me everywhere. When I got to work he would be standing
in front of the building. If I went to the supermarket he was there.
When I visited a friend I would come outside, and he would be sitting
somewhere on the street in his car watching me.

     I started getting threatening telephone calls from Ashly. So I
filed for a Restraining Order which really didn't help me. I learned
the hard way that it was a useless piece of paper. It wasn't worth
the ink, and paper used to print it on as far as Ashly was concerned.
I was filled with utter terror when I saw the statistics of women who
were murdered by men that they had Restraining Orders on.

     Things got so bad that I had to call my youngest brother, Marvine.
He was the only one of my brothers who wasn't married, and had a
family. He had no trouble staying with my daughter and I. He would
take me to and from work every day. As well as any other place I
needed to go. I guess you could say that he was like a bodyguard.
Needless to say, once my brother started doing this I didn't see
Ashly anymore. Yet, I was still in such a precarious situation.

     Marvine spent a lot of nights with Tanda and I. He was with us at
least four or five nights a week. There were times when he couldn't
be with us, and those were the times when I was most afraid. Even if
I didn't see him I knew that Ashly was lurking in the shadows of some
dark corner. Sometimes my mother would come over, and one of my other
brothers when Marvine couldn't be with us. Usually somebody was
always with my daughter and I.

     My mother pleaded with me to come live with her. But I wouldn't do
it. I liked having my own space and my privacy. I should have
realized it was all illusory on my part. The one valuable thing that
I didn't have was peace of mind. To me, next to good health, it was
more important than anything else in the world.

    While on my vacation I was at home one night putting up Christmas
decorations. Marvine and Tanda were watching television when the
telephone rang. My brother answered it in case it might be Ashly
trying to intimidate me. But it wasn't. "It's somebody from the
station, Tray," said Marvine. "It sounds like it's kind of urgent."
I took the receiver from him. It was Myrna.

    "Traya," she said with urgency in her voice, "do you think you can
come down here for a few minutes?" "What's wrong?" I asked her
curiously. "What's the matter, Myrna?" "We've got a serious problem
with one of the Cameramen," she told me. "I think he's been drinking
again. He's really acting rambunctious, Traya, and he says he'll only
talk to you." "Who is it?" I asked her, already knowing who it was.
"It's Frankie," she said calming down. "Okay," I replied. "I'll be
right there." I hung up the telephone.

    "What's going on?" asked Marvine curiously when I got off of the
telephone. "I don't know," I said. "It's Frankie again. I have to go
down there for a few minutes and talk to him." "Just let me get my
jacket," said my brother getting up from his chair. "No," I said.
"You stay here with Tanda. I won't be long."

    "Look, Sis," he said concerned, "you know that maniac is out there
somewhere." "I'll be alright, Marv," I assured him getting my
sweater, and the keys to his car. "I'll be back before you know it."
I ignored the worried look that was on his face. And always regretted
that I didn't listen to him and let him come with me.

    "Alright," he told me. "I'll give you a half an hour. If you're not
back by then I'm calling Connell, and Mark. Deal?" "It's a deal," I
said smiling at him. I left for the station which was only ten
minutes away. I figured my visit to the station would be an quick
one. Still, it was the last thing that I needed just before
Christmas.

    When I got outside I saw something strange. A dark-colored car with
black, tinted windows caught my eye immediately. I had never seen
that car on our street before. However, I shrugged it off as paranoia
because it could have been anybody's car. Ashly didn't drive a car
like that. He drove a red Mustang. So I got into Marvine's
car, started the engine, and headed for the T.V. station. All I had to
do was find out what Frankie's problem was. For a brief instant when
I looked into the rear view mirror I thought that someone was
following me. But I shrugged that off as paranoia, too.

    Frankie Dunlougher was a young man who was three years older than I
was. He let me know many times that he was attracted to me. Yet, I
wasn't interested in him. He was tall, dark, and handsome, too. He

wouldn't have a problem getting any woman he wanted. But he wanted me
which was largely his problem.

 I turned him down every time he asked me out on a date. After that
he turned to drinking during working hours, and acting ugly at times.
I couldn't seem to make him understand that I couldn't think of
getting into another relationship as long as Ashly was hanging
around. He was a serious problem that I had to get rid of first.
Needless to say, Frankie didn't care a damn about Ashly and wasn't
afraid of him. He offered to get rid of Ashly for me by any means
necessary. I didn't want to resort to criminality. But if I had
another chance to consider his offer......

 Frankie would have too many rum and cokes down at the bar on the
corner from the television station. He would come to work and cuss
everybody out for no reason. Our boss, Jack Harole, believed he was
one of the best Cameramen in the business. It was the only reason why
he hadn't been fired.

 When Frankie wasn't drinking he was very good at his job, and a very
sweet person. He told me that he did the things he did because he was
so frustrated with me not giving him a chance. When he got out of
hand we would go somewhere and talk. That night was no different. It
seemed like I was the only one who could put him back together so to
speak.

 After I alleviated things with Frankie's terrible behavior that
night I headed for my brother's car to go home. I noticed the same
dark-colored car with the black, tinted windows again. This time it
was parked next to Marvine's car. As I approached the car to get in
my heart started pounding in my chest.

 I hadn't gotten the door unlocked when an insidious hand covered my
mouth from behind me. I never had a chance to scream for help. My arm
was roughly twisted behind my back. The pain was excruciating.

 "You're coming with me, you bitch!" It was Ashly. He dragged me,
still covering my mouth, to his car and forced me inside it. It was
the same dark-colored car with the black, tinted windows. It wasn't
the car that he usually drove. I was terrified! He held onto the back
of my head by my hair, and drove the car with his other hand. My head
hurt like crazy! He was yanking and pulling my hair from behind.

 "Ashly!" I cried. "Please! Let me go! Please!" "Shut up! You
rotten, stupid bitch!" he spat at me through clenched teeth. "Where
are your no good brothers now? I told you that I was going to kill
you. Didn't I? But you didn't believe me. Well, I have your ass now,
and nobody is going to save you!"

"Ashly, please!" I begged him. "Don't hurt me! Please! You don't
want to do this! Think about Tanda!" "Shut up, you stinking bitch!"
he said nefariously. I kept quiet after that too scared to say
anything else that might make him really hurt me badly. From the way
that he spoke to me I could easily tell how much Ashly hated me. It
was something that I realized had always been there. He never really
loved me. Still,I thought that I might be able to quell his rage.

I knew without a doubt that he was going to kill me. I had to think
fast. I began to plead with him again. I said anything and everything
that I thought he wanted to hear. Especially that we could get back
together if he wanted to. But he wasn't falling for my lies.

I watched the street signs whiz by us until there were no more of
them. We were on the highway that headed out of town. I knew I was in
trouble. So quickly I put my hand on the door handle. I considered
jumping out of the speeding car to get away from him once he loosened
his grip on my hair. "I have to get out of here," I thought
fearfully. "If I don't he's going to kill me."

Before I could think about it any longer I hurriedly opened the car
door, and jumped out onto the road. He lost his grip on my hair, and
tried to grab me but he wasn't fast enough. I hurt my arm and my leg
when I jumped out of the car. I knew that something was broken by the
fall because of the pain. However, I managed to pull myself up. But
all I could do was crawl. One of my legs was broken. I saw Ashly put
the car in reverse. There wasn't another car in sight.

I thought that was strange at first. Until I saw the sign that read:
"Highway Closed For Repairs". I panicked! By that time I knew I
was going to die if no one came to my aid. I saw the car reverse
lights coming toward me. I desperately tried to drag myself away, but
I didn't get far. There was no way that I could've gotten away from
Ashly.

I was knocked to the side of the road when Ashly hit me with the
car on purpose. I couldn't move at all after that. I had no choice
but to lay there on the side of the road. "Oh, God!" I prayed
silently. "Help me, please! Don't let me die! Don't let this crazy
man take me away from my child."

"Traya," I heard the same strange woman's voice call to me for the
first time as I laid there on the ground. "Traya, it's time now. It's
your time." I thought the mysterious woman was telling me that it
was my time to escape that deranged lunatic.

The next thing I knew Ashly got out of his car. I saw him walking
slowly toward me where I lay on the ground. Also, I saw something

long and shiny in his hand. Thoughts were whirling around in my mind.
I couldn't stop thinking about my little girl. I thought, "How could
I have ever thought that I loved this monster?" "Come on, Traya," I
heard the woman's voice again. "It's your time."

Ashly straddled me as I laid there on the ground. "You stupid,
silly bitch!" he spat at me. His eyes had a crazed look in them. "No,
Ashly, please don't!" I pleaded. I felt a searing, hot pain in the
middle of my chest. Then another one, and another one until I stopped
counting them. My fighting was useless. I was being stabbed over and
over again. Then there was nothing but darkness.

I awoke in the hospital. I got out of the bed surprised that I
wasn't badly hurt. There was no pain. I walked into the hallway where
I saw my mother and my brothers. They were all crying. Marvine was
punching the walls enraged.

"Mom," I said to my mother, "what's going on? Why are you guys
crying?" But she never answered me and neither did my brothers. My
mind came back to what was going on around me. The Eulogy was over.

Everybody in the church formed a line so they could view the
woman's body again. There was more weeping. It was so sorrowful.
After that everyone got back into their designated cars, and returned
to my house. Coffee and cake were being served. I watched Tanda as
she retreated to her bedroom sobbing softly.

"I don't know what I'm going to do with this house she bought," I
heard my mother tell somebody. "I guess I'll have to sell it. Nobody
wants to stay here after something like this." "What?" I cried. "You
can't sell my house, Mom! Where will Tanda and I live? Why would you
do that?" *She has no right to sell my house,* I thought.

It took me two years to save enough money to buy a house for Tanda
and I. I was so proud of my accomplishment. Ashly insisted that
Tanda and I didn't need a house. And that I didn't need to own my own
home. I didn't listen to him. As far as he was concerned Tanda and I
didn't need anything or anybody but him.

Everyone was engaged in conversation. I walked over to a circle of
people so I could hear what they were talking about. "Maybe I can
join in the conversation," I thought. I found out that the people in
the circle were talking about me. "Traya," said the enigmatic woman's
voice, "we must leave here." "In a minute," I replied becoming
impatient. The person was rushing me away and I was beginning to get
annoyed.

"She was the best Associate Programmer I had," said my boss, Mr.

Harole. He was a short, stout, balding man who was very kind-hearted.
"Damn shame for something like this to happen." "I still can't
believe it," said Renee Yonkers. She was a woman I never liked
that I worked with. She was always jealous of me for reasons that I
never knew. And she could never hide her envy. It was speculated
among our co-workers that she had a thing for Frankie. I gathered
that was why she didn't like me.

   "There will never be another one like her," she added. "I'll miss
Traya that's for sure." "Me?!" I said surprised. "Why would you miss
me?"   I wondered where I was going that would cause her to miss me.
I knew that they had no reason to fire me. I was surprised to learn
that she liked me after all. You just never know about some people.

   I saw Frankie Dunlougher sitting in a corner of my living room
alone. He looked like he had just lost his best friend. I walked over
to him. "How are you doing, Frankie?" I asked him. He stared blankly
past me. I saw tears in his eyes.

   I saw my mother heading up the stairs so I followed her. She went
to Tanda's bedroom and knocked lightly on the door. "Come in," said
my little girl.

   "Oh, Tanda, honey," said my mother. "It's going to be alright.
You're coming to live with me. Okay?" "Yes, Grandmom," said Tanda
sweetly. "What?" I cried. "Why is my daughter going to live with you,
Mom?" "Your mother is in a nice place, sweetie," my mother told her.
"She's an angel now. And she can watch over you forever."

   "Mom, are you crazy?" I asked her. "I'm right here." "Let's go back
downstairs, honey," said my mother. "Okay?" "Okay, Grandmom," said my
little girl. They went back downstairs and I followed them. Some of
the guests were leaving by then.

   "We'll be back in the morning for the burial," Uncle Leon told my
mother. I was glad to see him. He was my father's only brother and my
favorite uncle. I hadn't seen him since my father died because he
lived so far away from us, nearly 2,000 miles. A lot of people left
to go home but some people spent the night. That was another custom
in our family before, and after a funeral, to put up as many
traveling relatives in our homes as we could.

   The following morning my house was filled again with people. The
Undertaker, Mr. Whims, performed his duty of organizing everyone into
their perspective cars. I got into the car with my mother and my
daughter. Before the procession to the cemetery began two police
officers came to the house. They wanted to talk to my mother. So they
came over to the car where we were.

"Sorry to intrude on your grief like this, Mrs. Norris," said one
of the officers. "But we wanted you to know that we've apprehended
Ashly Waring." "Yes," said the other officer. "And he's confessed to
murdering your daughter." "Thank God," said my mother with relief.

"Okay, Maam," said one of the officers, "that's all that we came to
tell you. Again we're sorry to intrude." "That's alright, officers,"
said my mother. "Thank you so much." They signaled for Mr. Whims to
proceed.

"My, God!" I thought. *"Is that what happened to me? I was at
my own funeral?"* All I could remember was Ashly attacking me and
waking up in the hospital. But I had been brutally and viciously
stabbed to death. "Now can we leave, Traya, honey?" asked the
strange, female voice. "Just a little longer," I told her. We arrived
at the cemetery. By then I knew that no one could see me or hear me.

Everybody got out of their cars and walked to the grave site. I
stood beside my mother, Tanda, my brothers and their families. I
looked at the beautiful tombstone. It read: *"Traya Mae Norris,
born August 8, 1961, died December 19, 1996. Beloved Mother,
Daughter, and Sister"*.

I was glad to know that so many people loved and cared about me.
And that I had touched their lives in some small way. I realized
Tanda would be alright. My mother and the other members of my family
would take good care of her. They would see her through the most
tragic and terrible Christmas of her young life. And one that she
would likely never be able to forget.

I hoped with all of my heart that neither Frankie nor Myrna would
blame themselves. Since they were the reason that Ashly had a chance
to get me alone and take my life. I was resolute that what happened
to me would have happened anyway, sooner or later. Evidently, it was
the way that I was meant to go.

I knew that Ashly would pay for what he did to my family and I,
too. "Traya, please," said the mysterious, female voice. "It's time
to go." "Yes," I agreed. "It is time for me to go. Isn't it? I can
leave now." As I looked down at my clothes I was wearing the same
ones that I had on the night that I was murdered, not the light blue
dress that I saw on the woman in the casket. I never saw her face,
only the dress and her hair. I didn't know it was me.

As I looked around me all of the people had vanished. I was
surrounded by nothing but big, white clouds. There was an elderly
lady with a strange glow around her all dressed in white standing
beside me. I realized that hers' was the voice that I had been

11

hearing. The voice that was trying to urge me to *move on*.

   I didn't recognize her at first. But as I looked closer I could see
that it was my beloved, paternal grandmother. She died when I was
twelve years old. And she was right. It was time for me to leave this
world. I hated to leave family, friends, and most of all my darling,
little girl behind. But I didn't belong in their world anymore. I
would live on in their memories forever, especially in Tanda's.

"THE   END"

Notes

Notes

Notes

Notes

Notes

Notes

Notes

Notes

Notes

Notes

Notes

Notes

Notes

Notes

Notes

Notes

Notes

Notes

Notes

Notes

Notes

Notes

Notes

Notes

Notes

Notes

Notes

Notes

Notes

Notes

Notes